For three-legged dogs everywhere ~ J.K.

For every one of my pets, past, present & future.
Each of you so very loved, each of you so very perfect ~ S.L.

tiger tales
5 River Road, Suite 128, Wilton, CT 06897
Published in the United States 2018
Originally published in Great Britain 2018
by Little Tiger Press
Text copyright © 2018 John Kelly
Illustrations copyright © 2018 Steph Laberis
ISBN-13: 978-1-68010-118-8
ISBN-10: 1-68010-118-8
Printed in China
LTP/1400/2214/0318

For more insight and activities, visit us at www.tigertalesbooks.com

What Do You Do if Your House is a Zoo?

by
John Kelly

Illustrated by
Steph Laberis

tiger tales

But what pet did I want? I just couldn't decide.

So on Monday, I put an ad in the local paper.

LITTLE BUMBLING NEWS

· CLASSIFIEDS ·

IN SEARCH OF . . .

Cave too stinky?
Friends won't stop snoring?
Then get away from it all at . . .
The Hibernation Hotel

Could you be the pet for me?

If so, contact me, Oscar, at:
99 Ice Cream Drive,
Little Bumbling

Looking for friends?
Join 'Our Cl...
Anyone we...
No joining f...

FOR SALE

For Sale!
(One careful owner)
· Emperor Flabulon Video Game
· The Windy Pirates DVD
· Penguin All-Stars Sticker Book

Rare!
"Hiss" Autographed LP.
Signed by all the band
...st on to...
...detail...

And on Tuesday . . .

. . . I received some replies!

The first one was on **VERY** fancy paper.

To whom it may concern,

You may address me as "Your Highness" or by my full title, Princess Cushion-Slasher Furball the Third.

If I am to grace your dwelling with my royal bottom, I shall require the following:

1. Lots of cushions or laps.

2. No other pets, especially dogs. (Goldfish are acceptable.)

3. My own 24-hour private entrance.

4. Fresh fish. Fresh cream. Fresh chicken. No cans!

Yours sincerely,

Princess

The next reply was **short** and **sweet** (but a little bit damp).

Hi! My name is Goldie!
I don't eat very much and I live
in a nice clean bowl . . . .
Hi! My name is Goldie!
I don't eat very much and I—
OOH!, LOOK!
A treasure chest!
Goldie xxx

And the last one had been **nibbled** on
by the sender!

MY NAME IS BILL. BILLY G. GRUFF.
AND BY MY BEARD I'M NOT FUSSY.
I'LL EAT ANYTHING.
GRASS, FLOWERS, HATS
IRES, CuPS, PENCILS,
CHAIR   N LINERS,
                                          OTBA
                          CHEESE, POTATO PEELINGS

This was going to be tough.
And it got even tougher, because on
Wednesday, the mail carrier brought more replies.

. . . the more confused I became!

There were so many animals,
the choice was making me **DIZZY!**

We're the meerkats! We'll keep you safe!

We'll PROTECT you from EVERYTHING.

Security guaranteed —
24 hours a day!

Greetings, tiny adorable human!
You're such a cutie!
I just want to pick you up,
cuddle you, and climb to the top
of the Empire State Building.
YOU will be the
perfect pet for me!

Hi! My name is Olive.
We could go for a nice long run
together and get away from everything.
Or we could just stick our heads
in the sand. I don't mind, really.
Please pick me! Olive xx

Greetings! I am Anthony.
This is my brother, Anthony, my other brother, Anthony,
and my 12,359 other brothers named Anthony. We live with my mom,
Queenie, but are quickly running out of space. Can we come
and live with you? We're neat and clean
and great at heavy lifting. xx

Heigh-ho! Henrietta here!
You sound like a WINNER!
I'm a winner, too!
Best in show
(three years in a row).
· Highest jumper
· Shiniest coat · Smoothest hooves
I'd love to be your pet (as long as you always let me win).

Space Monkey
Boo-Boo calling!
I'm looking for a place
to crash and somewhere to
test my new rocket.*
I blast off in search of
the banana planet next
Tuesday, and I can't wait
to be your pet!

*It's not dangerous at all.
It probably won't even blow
up this time.

WILF THE WOLF HERE.
I MAY BE LONG IN THE TOOTH
(AND A LITTLE BIT GRAY) BUT I CAN
STILL KEEP UP WITH THE PACK.

I MIGHT NEED A BIT OF A NAP
AFTERWARD, THOUGH.

BILL & BOB BEAVER

We're not just pets.
We're builders* extraordinaire!
No job too big.
Experts in gardening.
Water features a speciality!

*Looking for new
premises due to
unexpected flooding.

Name's Ollie. Can't wait to be your pet!
Likes: Juggling, ping-pong, filing, washing up, knitting.
Dislikes: Sitting still.
Bye-bye!

SNORT!

Bertram's the name.
China's the game!
I need somewhere to display my rather
delicate collection of precious antique
bone china.

Bertram.

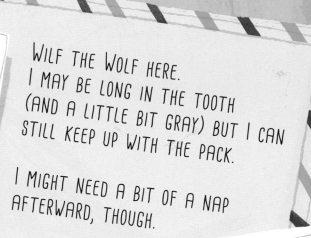

Why would Walter Whale (me)
make a wonderful pet?
Well, whales are no trouble at all.
All we need is a small lake, river, or Olympic-
sized swimming pool, and five tons of shrimp
every day (four as I'm currently on a diet).
Wettest wishes, Walter xx

And to make matters worse, on Thursday,
the meerkats arrived. They set up a security post
and wouldn't let Mom leave!

"I'll be late for work!" she cried until . . .

. . . Kingsley the gorilla kindly gave her a lift.

"That looks like fun!" I cried. "Can I go, too?"

"No way!" said Dad. "Why on earth did you invite them?"

. . . the Beaver Brothers appeared and built us
a backyard **WATER PARK**. This was more like it!
I was about to dive in when . . .

Walter Whale swam up
and turned Mr. and Mrs. Jones'
barbecue into a pool party!

"**Listen!**" said Dad as he blow-dried Mr. Jones' wig.

"No more animals!"

But they kept on coming—our house felt like a zoo!
Soon I was surrounded by pets, but not one
of them wanted to play with me.

In fact, our house was so full that we ended up sleeping in the yard. "Peace at last," sighed Dad, when

WHOOSH! CrUNCh! TINKLE!

we were woken by Space Monkey Boo-Boo crash-landing on the shed.

"THAT'S IT!" cried Mom. "They ALL have to go!"

But I don't think any of them was the pet for me.

Then on Monday, I found a letter I had missed!

It was **smelly, drooly,** and covered in **fur,**
but I opened it anyway.

Pick me!
I love you!
We've never met, but
I love you already!

My name is Rufus,
but I answer to: BAD DOG!
STOP THAT! and **GET**
OFF THAT CHAIR!

I like running (a lot),
and jumping, and rolling,
and balls, and mud, and chasing
cats, and running!
I'm very loyal and we'll be
best friends FOREVER.
Rufus xxx

P.S. I'll eat anything, but I would much rather eat your food.

And suddenly I realized that the pet for me isn't
the one who **I WANT** . . .

. . . it's THE ONE
WHO WANTS ME!

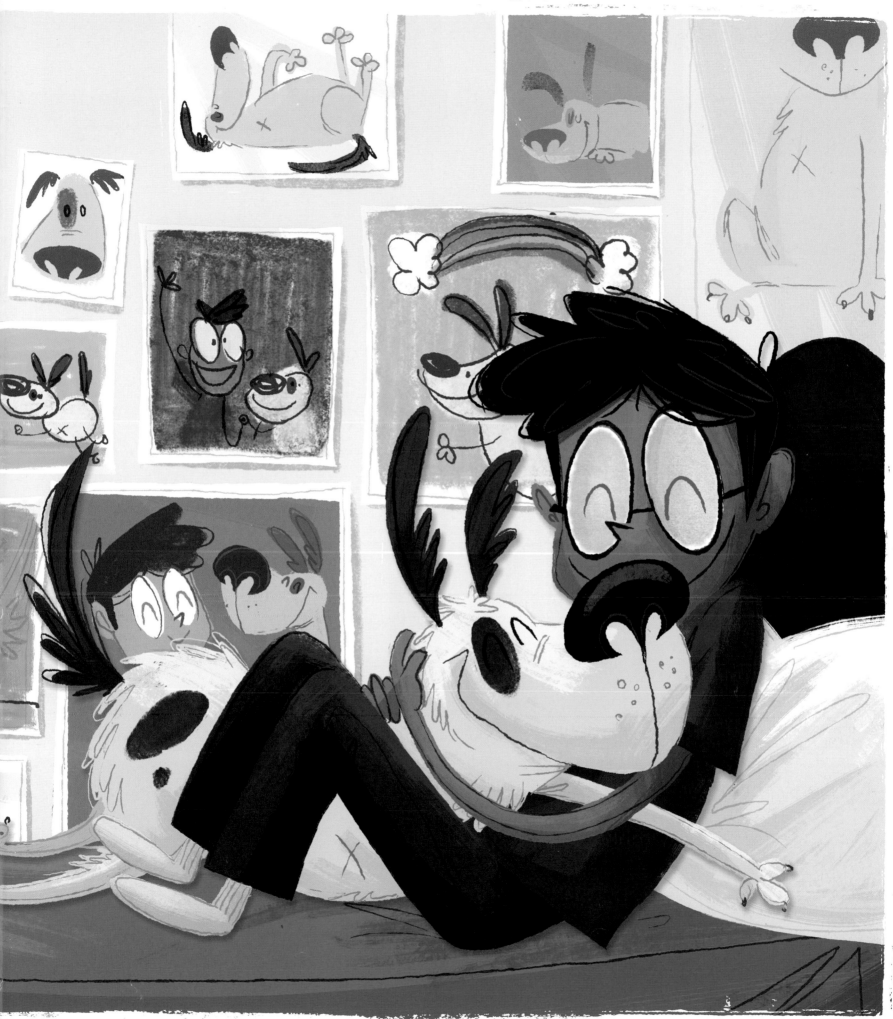